· Gordon ·

· Harold ·

· Percy ·

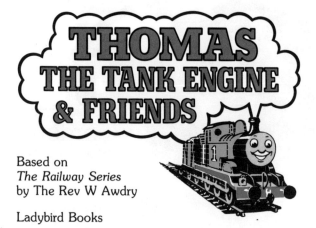

THOMAS THE TANK ENGINE & FRIENDS

Based on
The Railway Series
by The Rev W Awdry

Ladybird Books

Acknowledgment
*Photographic stills by David Mitton and Terry Permane
for Britt Allcroft (Thomas) Ltd.*

British Library Cataloguing in Publication Data
Awdry, W.
    Thomas comes to breakfast; Boco the Diseasel.—
    (Thomas the tank engine & friends).
    I. Title   II. Awdry, W. Diseasel   III. Series
    823'.914[J]   PZ7
    ISBN 0-7214-1031-6

Thomas comes to breakfast

Thomas comes to breakfast

Thomas the Tank Engine has worked his branch line for many years, and knows it very well.

"You know just where to stop, Thomas," laughed his driver. "You could almost manage it without me!"

Thomas had become conceited. He didn't realise that his driver was joking.

Later he boasted to the others. "Driver says I don't need him now."

"Don't be daft," snorted Percy.

"I'd never go without *my* driver," said Toby earnestly. "I'd be frightened."

"Pooh!" boasted Thomas. "I'm not scared."

"You'd never dare," said the other engines.

"I would then," boasted Thomas. "You'll see!"

Next morning the fireman came. Thomas drowsed comfortably in the shed as the warmth spread through his boiler. Percy and Toby were still asleep.

Thomas opened his eyes and then he suddenly remembered. "Silly stick in the muds," he chuckled. "I'll show them! Driver hasn't come yet, so here goes."

He cautiously tried one piston; then the other. "They're moving! They're moving!" he whispered. "I'll just go out, then I'll stop and 'wheeesh'. That'll make them jump!"

Very, very quietly he headed past the door.

Thomas thought that he was being clever, but really he was only moving because a careless cleaner had meddled with his controls. He soon found out his mistake.

He tried to 'wheeesh' but he couldn't. He tried to stop but he couldn't. He just kept rolling along.

"The buffers will stop me!" he thought hopefully, but the siding had no buffers. Thomas's wheels left the rails and crunched the tarmac. There was the station master's house!

Thomas didn't dare to look at what was coming next. The station master and his family were about to have breakfast.

"Horrors!" cried Thomas and shut his eyes.

There was a crash! The house rocked
and broken glass tinkled. Plaster peppered
the plates.

Thomas had collected a bush on his travels. He peered anxiously into the room through its leaves. He couldn't speak.

The station master was furious.

The station master's wife picked up her plate. "You miserable engine," she scolded. "Just look what you've done to our breakfast! Now I shall have to cook some more."

She banged the door. More plaster fell. This time, it fell on Thomas.

Thomas felt depressed. The plaster was tickly. He wanted to sneeze but he didn't dare in case the house fell on him. Nobody came for a long time. Everyone was much too busy.

At last workmen propped up the house with strong poles and laid rails through the garden.

Donald and Douglas arrived. "Dinna fash yerself, Thomas. We'll soon hae ye back on the rails," they laughed.

Puffing hard, the twins managed to haul Thomas back to safety.

Bits of fencing, the bush and a broken window frame festooned Thomas's front, which was badly twisted. He looked very funny.

The twins laughed and left him.
Thomas was in disgrace, but there was
worse to come.

"You are a very naughty engine,"
came a voice.

"I know, sir," said Thomas. "I'm sorry, sir." Thomas's voice was muffled behind his bush.

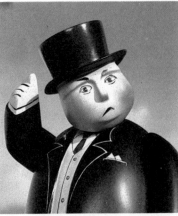

"You must go to the works and have your front end mended. It will be a long job," said the Fat Controller.

"Yes, sir," faltered Thomas.

"Meanwhile, a diesel railcar called Daisy will do your work."

"A d-d-diesel, sir? D-D-Daisy, sir?"
Thomas spluttered.

"Yes, Thomas," said the Fat Controller.
"Diesels *always* stay in their sheds till they
are wanted. Diesels *never* gallivant off to
breakfast in station masters' houses."

The Fat Controller turned on his heels,
and sternly walked away.

Boco the Diseasel

Boco the Diseasel

Bill and Ben are twin tank engines who live at the port near Edward's station.

Each has four wheels, a tiny chimney and dome, and a small squat cab.

The twins are kept busy pulling trucks for engines on the main line, and for ships in the harbour.

Their trucks are filled with china clay
dug from the nearby hills. China clay is
important. It is needed for pottery,
paper, paint and many other things.

One morning, they arranged some
trucks and went away for more. They
returned to find them all gone.

The twins were most surprised.

Their drivers examined a patch of oil. "That's a diesel," they said, wiping the rails clean.

"It's a what'll?" asked Bill.

"A *diseasel*, I think," replied Ben.
"There's a notice about them
in our shed."

"I remember, *'coughs and sneezles
spread diseasels'*," said Bill.

"Who had a cough in his smoke box
yesterday?" said Ben.

"Fireman cleared it, didn't he?" said Bill.

"Yes, but the dust made him sneeze: so there you are," said Ben, huffily. "It's *your* fault the diseasel came."

"It isn't!"

"It is!"

"Stop arguing, you two," said their drivers. "Come on! Let's go and rescue our trucks."

Bill and Ben were horrified. "But the diseasel will magic us away like the trucks!" they said.

Their drivers laughed. "He won't magic

us," they said. "We'll more likely magic him! Listen – he doesn't know you're twins, so we'll take away your names and numbers and then this is what we'll do..."

Bill and Ben chuckled with delight.
"Come on! Let's go!" they said eagerly.

Puffing hard, the twins set off on their
journey to find the diesel. They were
looking forward to playing tricks on him.

Creeping into the yard, they found the
diesel on a siding with the missing trucks.

Ben hid behind, but Bill went boldly alongside.

The diesel looked up. "Do you mind?" he asked.

"Yes," said Bill. "I do. I want my trucks, please."

"These are mine," said the diesel.
"Go away."

Bill pretended to be frightened.
"You're a big bully," he whimpered.
"You'll be sorry." He ran back and hid
behind the trucks on the other side.

Ben now came forward. "Truck stealer!" he hissed.

Then he ran away too and Bill took his place.

This went on and on till the diesel's eyes nearly popped out.

"Stop!" he begged. "You're making me giddy."

The two engines gazed at him. "Are there two of you?" he asked, in a daze.

"Yes, we're twins," chimed Bill and Ben.

"I might have known it," groaned the diesel.

Just then
Edward bustled
up. "Bill and
Ben, why are
you playing
here?" he said, crossly.

"We're *not* playing," protested Bill.

"We're rescuing our trucks," squeaked Ben.

"What do you mean?" asked Edward.

"Even *you* don't take our trucks without asking, but this diseasel did!" they both squeaked indignantly.

"There's no cause to be rude," said Edward. "This engine is a Metropolitan Vickers Diesel-Electric, Type 2."

The twins were abashed. "We're sorry Mr – er..." they stammered.

"Never mind," the diesel smiled. "Call me Boco. I'm sorry I didn't understand about the trucks."

"That's all right, then," said Edward. "Now off you go, Bill and Ben. Fetch Boco's trucks, then you can take this lot."

The twins scampered away. Edward
smiled. "There's no real harm in them,"
he said to Boco, "but they're maddening
at times."

Boco chuckled. "Maddening," he said,
"is the word."

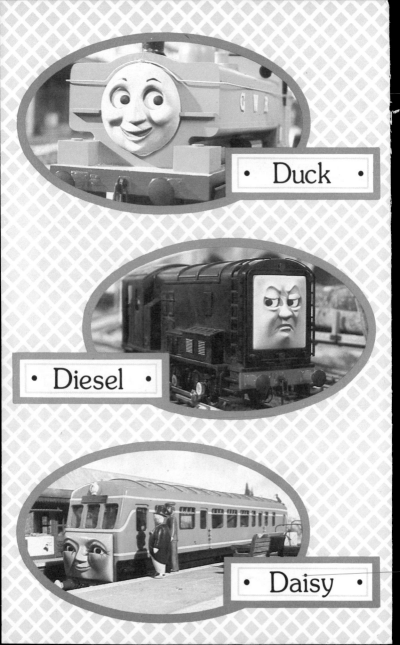

• Duck •

• Diesel •

• Daisy •